MY LiFe as POLLUTED Pond Scum

BOOKS BY BILL MYERS

Children's Series
McGee and Me! (12 books)

The Incredible Worlds of Wally McDoogle:
—*My Life As a Smashed Burrito with Extra Hot Sauce*
—*My Life As Alien Monster Bait*
—*My Life As a Broken Bungee Cord*
—*My Life As Crocodile Junk Food*
—*My Life As Dinosaur Dental Floss*
—*My Life As a Torpedo Test Target*
—*My Life As a Human Hockey Puck*
—*My Life As an Afterthought Astronaut*
—*My Life As Reindeer Road Kill*
—*My Life As a Toasted Time Traveler*
—*My Life As Polluted Pond Scum*

Fantasy Series
Journeys to Fayrah:
—*The Portal*
—*The Experiment*
—*The Whirlwind*
—*The Tablet*

Teen Series
Forbidden Doors:
—*The Society*
—*The Deceived*
—*The Spell*
—*The Haunting*
—*The Guardian*
—*The Encounter*

Adult Books
Christ B.C.
Blood of Heaven

MY LiFe as POLLUTED Pond Scum

BILL MYERS

WORD PUBLISHING
Dallas·London·Vancouver·Melbourne

MY LIFE AS POLLUTED POND SCUM

Copyright © 1996 by Bill Myers.

Managing Editor: Laura Minchew
Project Editor: Beverly Phillips

Unless otherwise indicated, Scripture quotations are from the *International Children's Bible, New Century Version*, copyright © 1983, 1986, 1988.

Quotations marked NKJV are from the New King James Version, copyright © 1979, 1980, 1982, Thomas Nelson, Inc., Publisher.

Library of Congress Cataloging-in-Publication Data

Myers, Bill, 1953–
  My life as polluted pond scum / Bill Myers.
    p. cm. — (The incredible worlds of Wally McDoogle)

  Summary: Thirteen-year-old Wally must learn to trust God when his Career Day assignment on the local water management facility leads him to a rumor of a lake monster and a real scheme that threatens the town.
  ISBN 0–8499–3875–9 (pbk.)
  [1. Pollution—Fiction. 2. Christian life—Fiction.
3. Humorous stories.]   I. Title.   II. Series: Myers, Bill, 1953–
Incredible worlds of Wally McDoogle ; #11.
PZ7.M98234Mytp 1996
[Fic]—dc20   96–8256
                                            CIP
                                            AC

Printed in the United States of America

98 99 00 QBC 15 14 13 12 11

For Debra Bell and Sigmund Brouwer—
co-laborers committed to young people.

All things work together for good to those who love God, to those who are the called according to His purpose.

—Romans 8:28 (NKJV)

Contents

Chapter 1

Just for Starters . . .

All right, all right, I learned my lesson. Do whatever you want to me. I promise I will never, *never* complain about anything ever again.

- Run over me with the offensive line of the Dallas Cowboys, and you won't hear a peep (maybe some snapping bones and tearing muscles, but no peeps).
- Make me watch *Barney* reruns the rest of my life, and you'll still not hear what I'm thinking (how can you, when my mind has been turned to oatmeal?).
- Force me to eat my little sister's cooking, and . . . well, all right, I'd speak up then, but only because poisoning people to death is frowned upon in some countries.

The point is, from now on, whenever anything bad happens to me, I'm keeping my mouth shut

and looking for ways to use that bad for good.
'Cause when you do that, cool things happen.

How did I get to be such a know-it-all about this?
As usual, I learned the hard way. . . .

It all started back in Ms. Muddlemucker's geography class. She was finishing up one of her
thrilling lectures on the chief exports of some
South American country:

> " . . . wheat, rye, oats, and beef. This can
> be attributed to the arid climate created
> by the winds as they cross over the moun-
> tains thereby losing much of their mois-
> ture and . . . "

See what I mean?

I don't want to say this woman is boring, but
my best friend, Wall Street, who wants to make
her first million by the time she's fourteen, has
been recording Ms. Muddlemucker's classes and
selling the tapes in drug stores right next to the
sleeping pill section. And she's making a killing.

But there are a couple of advantages to taking
Ms. Muddlemucker's class. First, we all get to
catch up on our sleep. And second, we get to par-
ticipate in something called . . .

CAREER DAYS.

Each year every member of her class gets to be some hotshot city official for forty-eight hours. We actually get to go down to their offices and do their jobs for two days. Depending on our assignment, we get to be anything from Police Commissioner to Fire Chief to Dog Catcher to you name it.

Pretty cool, huh?

Not only do we get out of school, but we also get to play golf all day long and take three-hour lunches and do all the other neat stuff government officials always do.

What was even cooler was I knew exactly what job I was getting. Yes sir, there was no doubt about it. I would be the highly esteemed and most honorable Wally McDoogle, Mayor of Middletown.

"How could you be so sure?" you're asking.

Just by doing a little planning . . .

The first step was to find out when they were holding Career Days. Once I knew that, I spent a whole week ahead of time trying to impress Ms. Muddlemucker. Major-league stuff, like handing in my assignments with writing she could actually read, doing extra credit reports on, what else, her beloved South America, and even making a special effort not to drool on my desk when I slept.

But that was only half of it. Since I figured God would probably also have some say in the matter, I spent the rest of my time trying to butter Him up.

For nearly two weeks I said grace at every meal, wore clean socks to church, and on the last Sunday, I even volunteered to help collect the offering.

Of course, that made Pastor Bergman just a little nervous, until I bumped into the candle stand and knocked it over. Then he got a lot nervous. Even that wouldn't have been so bad if it wasn't for that one lone candle that fell into my offering plate and caught all the checks and dollar bills and stuff on fire.

As I handed Pastor Bergman the smoldering plate, I tried to make a little joke about "*burnt offerings*," but he didn't seem to get it. Then again, maybe he did.

Anyway, the big day finally rolled around. After finishing another stimulating lecture on South America (Do you know meat is the number one export of Argentina? Do you care?), Ms. Muddlemucker closed her geography book and announced that it was time to make the Career Days assignments.

All right! Everyone suddenly woke up, and we all gave her our fullest attention.

"Now," she said, "I know many of you have your hearts set on a particular job, but not everyone can have the top position."

You can say that again, I thought. *Only us hard workers (and non-desk droolers).*

"Still, I'm sure you'll find each and every one of these jobs a challenge and an adventure. So without any further ado . . . " She picked up the list and began reading the names: "Cindy Bullhocker, Superintendent of Schools."

Mild applause.

"Delbert Dillwood, City Treasurer."

More of the same.

She continued down the list until she got to Opera, my other best friend who got his name 'cause of his love for classical music. "And Opera," she said, "you'll be the Assistant Mayor."

All right! I thought. *If he's my assistant, we'll be able to hang out together!*

She continued rattling off a few more names until she came to Wall Street. "And finally, Wall Street, you will be our city's Mayor!"

"Yes!" Wall Street cried, giving Opera a high five. "Mayor of Middletown! All right!"

Everybody clapped. Everybody but me. It's hard to clap when your body's gone into traumatic shock.

"Ms. Muddlemucker, Ms. Muddlemucker," my hand shot up faster than that of some second grader having to go to the bathroom.

"Yes, Wally?"

"There must be some mistake."

"I don't think so."

"What about me?"

"Didn't I call your name?"

"No ma'am." (That extra respect stuff always gets them.)

"Oh, I'm sorry," she said, looking back down at the list.

I took a deep breath and forced myself to relax. Already I was feeling a little sorry for Wall Street. Poor kid. It's tough to have your hopes built up like that, only to have them dashed to smither—

"Oh, here we go," Ms. Muddlemucker said, looking up with a smile. "You're right, I did make a mistake."

A wave of relief washed over me.

"Wally, you will be in charge, let's see . . . ah, here we go. Wally McDoogle will be in charge of the Water Management Facility."

I blinked.

"Wally?"

I blinked twice. Then, after about a minute, I decided it would be a good time to start breathing again.

"Wally, are you all right?"

"I'm sorry," I croaked. "I thought you said 'Water Management Facility'?"

"That's right," she grinned. "You'll be in charge of managing and recycling all of our city's water and sewage."

"Sewage," I choked.

"Sewage," she grinned.

* * * * *

"They put you in charge of what?" My older brother Brock laughed so hard that he launched a bite of semichewed raw potato across the table. (It would have been a cooked potato, but it was my little sister's turn to make dinner.)

"Don't laugh," Bert, my other brother, laughed. "Maybe he can get us like free water samples or something."

"Free samples!" Brock laughed even harder, then suddenly he stopped. "Hey, maybe you're right."

Unfortunately, he was serious. Unfortunatelier, they both were. Unfortunateliest, when it comes to IQs, neither of my twin brothers has one. (I pray every night that it's not genetic.)

"Listen, Sweetheart," Mom said, trying her best to do the Mom thing for me, "I know it's not exactly what you expected, but I'm sure there's some very good reason for it."

"Yeah," I muttered, "God doesn't like the way I take up the offering."

"No, I'm serious," she said. "Instead of being discouraged about it, you should trust the Lord. He has a way of turning our disappointments into something good."

"I trust Him," I said.

"Then you should be content to bloom wherever He plants you."

"You'll certainly have the fertilizer for it there," Dad snickered.

There was more laughter (and jet-propelled potatoes).

"Don't you pay any attention to them," Mom said. "Besides, look at all the opportunities you'll have to learn about ecology and recycling."

Good ol' Mom, always looking on the bright side of things. As if to prove my point, she turned to my little sister Carrie and asked, "Sweetheart, will you pass some more of those delicious green beans you made?"

"They're not green beans," Carrie explained.

"Oh really?" Mom said, giving them a doubtful look. "What are they?"

"Hot dogs. They were just a little moldy, and I overcooked them some."

I glanced at my plate and breathed a sigh of relief. By their texture and taste, I was afraid I'd been eating earthworms rolled in kitty litter.

Mom forced a smile. "On second thought, maybe I better save room for dessert. What are we having?"

"Boiled ice cream."

"Then again, another hot dog might be just what I need."

Dad glanced up at me from his dinner plate. "Well, I for one am very happy for you, son."

"You are?"

"Absolutely. Getting out in those lakes and ponds, working with your hands. It should make a real man out of you."

"If the smell doesn't kill you," Brock laughed.

Everyone joined in, but Dad was serious. You see, making me into a real man was like his major life project. He started getting nervous way back last year when I told him I wanted to be a writer. Ever since then, strange things have started showing up in my bedroom. Vitamins, protein drink mixes with blenders, weight-lifting machines. In fact, just last week there was a form about joining the Marine Corps. Luckily, they don't take thirteen-year-olds.

"What exactly does a Water Management Facility do?" Carrie asked.

"It's more than just a facility," I explained. "It takes care of all the lakes, ponds, and reservoirs in our area."

"Even the ones up in the woods?" Burt asked.

"Like Knox Lake?" Brock added. There was a certain glee in his voice.

Mom looked at them. "What's up guys?"

"Everyone knows Knox Lake is where that giant monster lives," Burt explained.

"Oh that," Mom said, trying to cover it with a laugh but not doing a great job of it. "I've heard those rumors too. It's just a toxic dump site that's been sealed off. Don't tell me you actually believe those stories."

"I don't," Brock said, "but all the people who have seen it sure do."

"And don't forget the ghost," Burt added.

"Ghost?" Carrie asked, her little impressionable voice already starting to tremble.

"That's right," Burt said. "Some nights when the moon is full, people claim you can see a ghost with glowing hair standing on the shore, calling the monster to the surface."

A silence fell over the table. Even Mom was looking a little uneasy.

But not me. I was looking a lot uneasy. Having no idea what tomorrow would bring, but remembering my knack for always being in the wrong place at the wrong time, I opened my mouth and started shoveling in Carrie's cooking as fast as I could. After all, it's hard to be killed by giant monsters and glowing ghosts if you've already died from food poisoning.

Chapter 2

First Impressions

Thinking about tomorrow made it a little hard to get to sleep. Not that I was expecting to run into underwater monsters or glowing ghosts. With any luck I'd be cooped inside the Water Management Facility and never even get up to Knox Lake. Then, again, we all know about my luck . . . which is exactly why I couldn't get to sleep.

Then there were Mom's words. "If you really trust God, then you should bloom wherever He plants you." Right. I was supposed to believe that God was using this crummy situation for my best? I don't know. If this was for my best, I'd hate to see what was for my worst.

Anyway, I decided to do what I always do when I want to think things over. I reached for ol' Betsy, my laptop computer, and started another one of my superhero stories. . . .

K-ZING K-ZING K-ZING

Great Scott, another blast of photon-powered green peas have been fired at the spaceship. But such distractions are of little concern to the handsomely heroic Tidy Guy. Checking the rearview mirror to make sure his hair hasn't been mussed, our good guy cranks his space-craft to starboard (a fancy word for left or right, I can never keep them straight) and the deadly vegetables fly past.

Yet it is only the beginning of the attack, as the vile villain Veggie-Man reloads his Salad Shooter and swoops in for another assault.

K-ZING K-ZING K-ZING
 K-ZING K-ZING K-SPLAT

It's the *k-splat* that gets our good guy. Suddenly his windshield is covered with more goo than a baby's highchair after mealtime. But it's not the goo that bothers him, it's the unorganized way that the smashed peas are scattered across the glass.

As a neat freak, disorganization has always made Tidy Guy crazy. Why just last Saturday he had spent the entire day organizing the gravel in his driveway. Then there was last night's spaghetti. He couldn't go near the table until Mom had taken the noodles out of the bowl and carefully laid them out in straight lines on the table. (Talk about an eating disorder.)

In any case, before he can stop himself, Tidy Guy has thrown open his cockpit and climbed out onto the nose of his spacecraft to carefully reorganize the peas. Then, suddenly:

BEEP BEEP BEEP
BEEP BEEP BEEP

He reaches for his pocket pager just as Veggie-Man swoops by. "Hey, Tidy," he calls, "is that your beeper or mine?"

Tidy Guy unsnaps his pager from his belt and takes a look. "It's mine," he shouts. "Can you wait a minute?"

"I'd love to," Veggie-Man calls. "But I should be heading home."

"What's the rush?"

"I promised my dad I'd wax the family starship before the next meteor shower."

"Well, all right," Tidy Guy shrugs. "If you have to."

"Sorry."

"No sweat. And hey, thanks for the practice, Veg. It was great."

(And you thought Veggie-Man was a real bad guy. Of course, if you had read *My Life As an Afterthought Astronaut,* you'd know he'd already been turned into a good guy. But enough shameless promotion. Back to our story.)

After waving a fond farewell (and with the quiet assurance that more *Afterthought Astronaut* books might get sold), our hero pulls out his cordless phone and calls the number on his pager.

The voice on the other end is faint and full of static.

"Hello?" it answers.

"Hi, this is Tidy Guy. I'm returning your call."

"Tidy Guy, thank goodness you've called. help your need We."

Our hero frowns. "Pardon me?"

"We your need help! your We help need!"

"I'm sorry, your words are all scrambled."

"help your need We! your need help We!"

Sensing somebody might need his help (don't try this deep thinking at home, folks), Tidy Guy reaches for his Acme Unscrambler (sold at superhero stores everywhere) and turns it on. Instantly the words come in clear:

"We need your help! We need your help!"

"Who is this? Who needs my help?"

"We're from Planet Getalife. We're under attack."

"Who is attacking you? And why is your transmission all scrambled?"

"It's him. him It's..."

But the voice is fading again. The transmission grows so weak that even the Unscrambler doesn't help.

"Chaos...he attacking us is."

A cold chill shivers through our hero's body. While checking to make sure his goosebumps are perfectly lined up, Tidy Guy realizes why the words are scrambled. His archrival Chaos Kid is once again on the loose. As the baddest

of bad guys, Kid's sole purpose in life
is to spread chaos and disorder
throughout the universe.

"us Help...su pleh."

Now even their letters are being
scrambled.

It is time for action. Quickly
checking his coordinates, Tidy Guy
discovers Getalife is just two blocks
and a couple thousand light-years
away. Dropping his spacecraft into
hyperneat, he races off to help. Who
knows what mean-spirited mix-ups his
obnoxious antagonist is organizing.
What traumatic turnabouts he is con-
templating. Or how many terrible and
untidy tongue twisters I can work in
before this section is over. And then,
just when you're about to sprain your
mouth...

I hesitated. I wasn't sure where my story was
going or what would happen next. But that was
okay. Why should Tidy Guy's life be any different
from mine? I saved the story and shut ol' Betsy
down. Little did I know that in just a few short
hours my life would be even stranger and more
chaotic than Tidy Guy's.

* * * * *

At first glance you wouldn't know Mr. Snavely
was sanity impaired (even though it was obvious
he and Steve Urkel shopped for clothes at the same
place and Mr. Snavely seemed to be sporting more
than the usual number of pocket protectors). Still,
as he showed me around his one-man operation,
he seemed pretty normal.

"As you can see, the Water Management Facility
is fully automated, allowing one person to monitor the entire operation." He pointed to a wall of
TVs. "These screens keep an eye on the lakes and
reservoirs in the system . . . starting down here
at the filtration pools where the city's wastewater
is treated and purified, and going all the way up
here to Knox Lake."

"Knox Lake?" I asked.

"That's right. Of course because of its high level
of toxicity, that lake is restricted, so—"

"Except to monsters and ghosts," I pretended to
laugh.

He slowly turned to me.

I gave a weak little smile to show it was a joke.

He cranked up his own nervous version of a grin.
"Now Wallace," he said, "you certainly don't believe
those silly rumors, do you?"

"No, sir," I said. But it was obvious my answer
was as fake as his grin.

He continued to stare at me like I might know something I shouldn't. I forced another smile and, after fidgeting a hole in the floor with the toe of my shoe, I figured it might be a good time to change the subject. "What are all those meters below the screens for?" I asked.

He turned back to the monitors. "Those gauges display the water levels. If a certain level is too low, we raise it; if it's too high, we lower it."

He turned back and caught me still staring at the Knox Lake screen. "Unless of course it's Knox Lake," he said evenly. "With so many toxins, it would never do to drain that, would it?"

"No, sir," I said, continuing to dig my shoe toward China.

"Wouldn't want to endanger any downstream life, now would we?" He cranked up his grin even wider. "Not with our beloved Middletown right below it."

I nodded. Was it my imagination or had the room gotten like a hundred degrees hotter?

I looked back at the monitor. For a haunted lake it seemed pretty normal. Just your average lake in the hills surrounded by your average woods and, of course, your average ten-foot-high fence with barbed wire so nobody can get near it.

I glanced back at Mr. Snavely, who was still staring at me. I had a ton more questions about the

lake but figured I might wait until a little bit later
. . . like the year 2039.

I changed the subject.

"What do you do if the lakes and reservoirs
get too high?" I asked. "Or too low. How do you
raise them or lower them?"

He pointed to one of the monitors. In the corner
of the screen there were a bunch of pipes and stuff.
"See these valves?" he asked.

I nodded.

"Each lake has them. If there's a problem, I hop
on the motorbike parked outside and head up to
the lake where I can either open or close the valves
as necessary. From this location I can reach any
reservoir in the system in less than thirty minutes."

Again I nodded. Everything seemed simple
enough. Except for the staring part. He just
kept on doing it. Ever since I mentioned Knox
Lake, the guy had definitely gotten weird in a
Freddy Krueger kind of way.

Then, without notice, he spun around and
headed toward his office. "Come with me, young
Wallace," he said. "There's something I want to
show you."

Hanging out with this guy was definitely not
high on my top-ten list of things to do, but I saw
no other choice. Besides, if I didn't bring up Knox

Lake again, there was a chance he might actually become more human.

As I entered his office, I spotted a giant tree branch on his desk. It was pretty stupid looking with dried moss and old pine cones and stuff hanging from it. Since I hadn't exactly hit it off with him earlier, I figured I'd give it another try by using my world-famous McDoogle small talk. Unfortunately, my mouth was running before my brain got in gear.

"Hey," I said, pointing at the monstrosity, "what's that hunk of junk for?"

"That's my Environmentalist of the Year Award," he said as he tenderly picked it up. "My pride and joy."

I swallowed hard wondering if I should be getting my own trophy, "The McDoogle Open Mouth Insert Foot Award." But Mr. Snavely had barely noticed. Instead, he carefully stroked his treasure and began muttering, "After all these years of service, . . . this is all I have to show for it." His voice grew darker as he lost himself in thought. "Never paid what I'm really worth, . . . always taken for granted. . . . " Now he was staring out into space, "always having to put up with those stupid sewer jokes. . . . "

I don't want to say this guy was mentally disturbed, but I did catch myself glancing over at the coatrack wondering where he hung his straitjacket.

Then, suddenly remembering I was in the room, he looked to me and cranked up another fakey grin. "Say, Wallace, this is the time I usually make coffee. What do you say? Can you handle it?"

"Yes, sir."

"The kitchen is next door. Just go through the monitoring room. You can't miss it."

I nodded and headed out the door, grateful to put as much distance between us as possible. (I would have preferred to go to Colombia for the coffee beans, but for now the kitchen would have to do.)

Of course I didn't know anything about making coffee, but why bother Dr. Psycho with details. I figured it was like making hot cocoa. Heat up some water, throw in a dozen tablespoons (I like my hot chocolate on the sweet side), and there you have it.

So, thirty seconds later, I was in the kitchen trying to dissolve a half pound of coffee in a tiny little mug. It was then that I heard the shouting. Lots of it.

I looked up and realized it was coming from an air vent right above my head. The air vent leading directly to Mr. Snavely's office.

"I know I said next month," he was shouting.

"But with the stupid kid here, I have a perfect alibi. Everyone will believe it's his fault."

Now, I know it's not cool to eavesdrop, but I couldn't help myself. Especially when I figured that the "stupid kid" he was referring to was someone I happen to be very close to.

"No," his voice echoed in the air shaft, "you have to do it tomorrow. Tomorrow or we have no deal. No, don't worry about the lake. I'll go up there tonight and take care of it. You just make sure you have the money with you. No! It's tomorrow or nothing!" With that, there was a loud bang as he slammed the receiver down.

Maybe my imagination was working overtime, but something didn't sound right. And it sounded like it would be even less right by tomorrow. I didn't know what to do. I glanced down at the coffee. It was the thickness of chocolate pudding, which I figured was probably strong enough.

I decided to play it cool and head back to his office to get more information. But as I crossed through the monitor room I couldn't resist the temptation to glance at the Knox Lake video screen.

I wished I hadn't.

In the middle of the monitor, out toward the center of the lake, there was some major swirling and churning going on. I fought back my uneasiness and stepped closer for a look. In the middle of all the spinning water, a giant, black head began to emerge. And around that, a dozen swirling tentacles.

But that was only half of it.

The head and tentacles started moving toward the distant shore. It was hard to make out because of all the spray and mist, but standing on that distant shore was a large, glowing something. A large, glowing something with blazing, bright hair.

I tried to swallow, but it's hard to swallow when your mouth has turned into the Sahara Desert.

"Wallace!" The shout from the office made me jump. "Wallace, where's that coffee?"

Not taking my eyes from the screen, I slowly backed out of the room and into Mr. Snavely's office. Unfortunately, I didn't see the garbage can next to his door until I had stepped into it.

No problem, except that I couldn't seem to get my foot out of it and started stumbling backward.

Even that was no big deal, until I glanced over my shoulder and saw Mr. Snavely directly in my path, his eyes widening in terror.

"Walla—"

That was about all he got out before I crashed into him—coffee and all.

The good news was we both landed in a chair.

The bad news was the chair had wheels.

We zipped across that room at just under the speed of sound. It was then I had the nifty idea to stick out my hands and try to slow us down. Unfortunately, there were only two things to grab hold of.

The first was his floor lamp,

RRIIIP
CRACKLE . . . SPARK . . . SPARK . . .

which did nothing to slow us down, although it was definitely a shocking experience.

CRACKLE . . . SPARK . . . CRACKLE . . .
"YEOOOWWW!"

The second was his bookcase, which was a pretty good idea except for the part where it ripped away from the wall and came crashing down on top of us.

K-THUNK!

So there we were, two guys in a chair with a cup of pudding-thick coffee, a shorting lamp, and a huge bookcase (complete with a thousand books on water management), all rolling toward a very unfriendly looking desk until, finally,

K-THUD!

we hit it.

After the usual moanings and groanings, I dug myself out of the wreckage of twisted lamp, broken bookcase, and a gazillion books, only to discover there were little pieces of tree limb, moss, and pine cones scattered everywhere. I threw a glance to the desk and went cold. Besides completely destroying Mr. Snavely's office, I had managed to totally demolish every square inch of his prized environmentalist award.

Below me, I could feel Mr. Snavely digging and clawing his way out. When he finally emerged, my pudding coffee was smeared all over his face.

I tried to ease the tension by smiling and making a little joke. "So, do you want some cream and sugar with that face?"

He didn't laugh. In fact, he didn't say a word. But if looks could kill, I should have taken the day off and done a little casket shopping.

Chapter 3

Close Encounters of the Weirdest Kind

"You're crazy," I yelled. "No way am I going up to Knox Lake."

"Come on," Wall Street said. "What are you afraid of?"

I thought for a moment, then in my bravest and most manly voice cried, "Everything."

Wall Street and Opera exchanged glances. Things weren't going well. Not well at all. It was the end of the day, and I had called them over to my house for an emergency meeting of Dork-oids Anonymous, of which I, of course, am the lifetime president. I needed their help in making a decision. Should I go back to the Water Management Facility tomorrow and face whatever trap Mr. Snavely was setting for me, or should I call in sick and opt for living a few more years?

A no brainer, right?

Well, not exactly. Not when you involve Wall Street and money. Just as soon as I mentioned the lake and assured her I had actually seen something on the monitor, her cash register brain went into overtime. Immediately she changed the subject and started talking about the three of us going to the lake and checking out the monster.

"It's our civic duty," she said. "The only honorable course of action," she insisted. "Besides, if there's really a monster, think of the millions we could make if we caught it and sold it to the zoo."

"I don't know." Opera sounded reluctant as he popped open his second bag of Chippy Chippers, those wonderful, extra-crispy, deep-fried artery pluggers that he's so fond of eating. (Along with any other junk food he can get his pudgy little pinkies on.)

"But we'd make a fortune," Wall Street insisted.

Still no takers.

It was time to break out the big guns, to go for the jugular, to bravely go where no money-grubber had gone before. She turned directly to Opera and asked, "Do you have any idea how many bags of potato chips you would be able to buy with the money we made?"

Opera glanced down at the bag in his hand. Then he looked over at me. But seeing the fear and concern in my eyes, he did what any true-blue friend would do. He closed up the bag, fought back a belch, and asked, "So when do we go?"

"Guys," I said as I rose to my feet. They looked at me, waiting for more. Okay, fine. They wanted more, I'd give them more. "Guys, guys, guys, guys."

They continued to stare. So much for my debating skills.

I tried another approach. "Listen, first of all, Knox Lake is not the problem. Surviving whatever Snavely's going to do to me tomorrow, that's the problem. And second . . . second . . . " Unfortunately I didn't have a second, so I improvised. "And second, it's almost spring break. Do you have any idea what a drag it is to be eaten by a monster just before spring break?"

I could tell by the embarrassed silence that I must have really stumped them.

At last Wall Street cleared her throat. "You're right, Wally," she said. "We've been incredibly selfish." She turned to Opera, "How could we have been so spoiled and self-centered?"

"Lots of practice?" he suggested.

She shook her head. "I'm serious. I mean, here we are, thinking only about ourselves." She turned back to me. "Wally, when you're right, you're right."

"I am?" I asked suspiciously.

"Absolutely. Say, can I borrow your phone book?"

I nodded, feeling a wave of cautious relief slowly wash over me.

She grabbed the book and started flipping through the pages, looking up a number. "That's why it's so important that we see that monster now," she said, "and not a second later."

"What?!" (So much for cautious relief.)

She looked up and, seeing my expression, patiently explained. "You're afraid if you go to work tomorrow, that somehow Mr. Snavely's going to hurt or maybe even kill you, right?"

"Right."

"If he does, there will be a big investigation at the facility. And since Knox Lake is part of that facility, they'll probably go up there and discover what's really in that water, right?"

"Right . . . "

She pulled a cellular phone out of her pocket and began to dial. "So everyone will know what's up there but you, 'cause you'll already be dead."

I frowned. "So . . . "

"So it's completely selfish and unfair for everybody else to know what's in that lake, except you."

Whatever safety I'd felt was rapidly slipping away. "Meaning . . . "

"Meaning, we have to find out what's up there now, today, before you die tomorrow."

I opened my mouth to argue, but no words came.

Not even a thought . . . except that maybe Wall Street should forget being a business tycoon and take up being a politician.

"Hello, Middletown Taxi?" She spoke into the phone and began negotiating with the taxi company about how much they would charge to take us up to the lake.

I looked first to her, and then to Opera, who was busy plowing back into his bag of chips. Yes sir, what a treat it was to know I had friends willing to go to any expense to look out for my welfare.

"Hey, Wally?" Wall Street asked. "Do you have a twenty to pay for the fare?"

Well, any expense, as long as it was mine.

* * * * *

Fifty-five minutes and twenty-four seconds later the three of us climbed out of the taxi. (Keeping track of time is important when you've only got a few hours left to live.) Wall Street had barely paid the driver my twenty before the cabbie gunned his engine and pealed out. Rocks and gravel spit in all directions as he raced down the deserted, tree-covered road as fast as he could.

"You think he knows something we don't?" Opera asked nervously.

"No," I said, watching the car disappear into the

distance. "I think he knows exactly what we know."
I turned to Wall Street. "So how are we going to
get back?"

She patted the cellular phone in her pocket. "I've
got his number. When we're ready to go home, I'll
just call and he'll come pick us up."

"If there's an *us* left to pick up," Opera said,
glancing around and giving a quiet shudder.

I nodded and looked into the dark, forbidding
woods that surrounded us. "Maybe you should
have gotten the number for the nearest funeral
home instead."

We stood a moment in the silence, each wondering what we'd gotten ourselves into. The sun
was just starting to set as we stood all alone in
the deserted foothills above our town . . . all alone
except, of course, for the wild animals, underwater
monsters, and glowing ghosts.

"Well, there's the path to the lake." Wall Street
pointed.

"Yeah," Opera said.

"Yeah," I said.

But, of course, none of us moved.

"I suppose we better get started."

"Yeah," Opera said.

"Yeah," I said.

Ditto in the moving department.

Then, after a deep breath, Wall Street braced

herself and started off. A moment later Opera followed. But for some reason, I couldn't seem to get my legs to move. I guess they had this thing about wanting to stay attached to my body and about wanting that body to live just a little while longer.

"Come on," Wall Street called over her shoulder. "We've only got a little daylight left."

I let out a heavy sigh and started forward. "All right," I called. "But if we die, you're going to live to regret it."

I'm not sure how long we hiked, but the deeper we got into the woods, the darker it got. And the darker it got, the more the place gave me the creeps, until suddenly . . .

Wall Street froze. "Listen," she whispered. We all stopped and grew silent.

click click click . . . click . . . click click

"What is that?" she asked.

We strained to listen. Something was tapping— making a strange brushing, clicking sound. It was faint, but there was no missing it. And the more we listened, the louder it grew.

Click . . . Click Click . . . Click Click Click . . .

"Sounds like . . . " Opera tilted his head to listen more carefully. "Sounds like some sort of code."

Wall Street nodded.

I continued listening, but it was getting harder and harder to hear over my pounding heart.

"Someone is trying to communicate with us," Wall Street whispered.

"Someone or some*thing*," Opera shivered.

CLICK CLICK . . . CLICK . . .

CLICK CLICK CLICK

It grew louder. Quickly our eyes scanned the surrounding trees, the bushes, everywhere— desperately looking for something. But what?

It was getting too dark to see a thing.

"Okay," Wall Street whispered. "Let's keep going. Let's see if it follows us."

Cautiously, we started forward. But with each step we took, it grew louder and louder. Whatever it was was nearly on top of us and *still* we couldn't see it. What was it? What did it want?

And then, just when our panic was at an all-time high, Wall Street spotted it. "Wally!"

I spun around to face her. She was staring at my feet. Well, not exactly my feet, more like my legs.

CLICK CLICK . . . CLICK CLICK CLICK

To be more specific, my knees.

CLICK . . . CLICK CLICK . . . CLICK

"It's your knees!"

"My knees?" I cried, jumping back.

"Yes." She started to laugh. "It's your knees knocking together."

I looked down. She was right. I was so scared, my knees were slam dancing into each other.

Everyone groaned. But before the humiliation could be piled on too high, we heard another sound. The loud snapping of twigs.

It was right behind us!

We spun around just in time to see a bright glowing object, about the size of a human, flying directly at us. Being the cool and courageous types we were, we did what any cool and courageous types would do. We twirled around and raced down the path screaming for our lives:

"AUGH . . . " That was Wall Street screaming.

"AUGHHHH . . . " That was Opera screaming.

"AUGHHHHHH"-*CLUNK,* "AUGHHHHHH"-*CLUNK,* "AUGHHHHHH"-*CLUNK.* That was me screaming and running into a few trees along the way.

In about 3.2 seconds we had reached the fence
that surrounded the lake. Since none of us felt any
great desire to stick around and become a "Happy
Meal" for a ghost, we turned to the right and
ran along the fence.

Well, Opera and Wall Street turned to the right
and ran along the fence. I forgot the turning part
and ran *into* the fence.

K-BAM!

And then I sorta got caught and tangled up in
it.

RATTLE, RATTLE, RATTLE

"I'm stuck," I cried. "I'm stuck!"

Opera and Wall Street spun around and raced
back. "It's your pants," Wall Street shouted. "Your
pants! They're hung up!"

I threw a look back into the woods. The snapping and cracking was quickly approaching. The
thing was still bearing down on us. Any second it
would emerge and—

"Go on," I shouted. "Save yourselves!"

"No!" Wall Street yelled as she began pulling.
"If you die, we all die!" (Although I appreciated
the thought, I didn't find it very comforting.)

They pulled on me harder, and harder some more, until . . .

RRIIIIP.

I was free. Well the *I* part of me was free. The pants part wasn't so lucky. They were still attached to the fence. I staggered to my feet, just me and my Fruit of the Looms, when suddenly, a bright light flashed down on us from above.

At first I hoped I had died, and it was an angel coming to take me to heaven. Unfortunately, I wasn't that lucky.

"What's going on down there?"

Wall Street and Opera froze. But I recognized the voice. It belonged to Mr. Snavely. I peered into the light. He was standing on a levee about fifteen feet above the lake and holding a giant flashlight. Beside him were a bunch of valves and stuff.

"Who's there?" he demanded.

"It's me," I shouted. "Wally McDoogle." I threw a look over my shoulder to see how many milliseconds we had before we became ghost kill. But, strangely, whatever had been chasing us had suddenly disappeared.

"Wallace?" Mr. Snavely called. "Wallace, what are you doing here?"

"We just came to do a little exploring," I called.

"Exploring? Tonight?"

"Yes, sir."

"In your underwear?"

"It's a long story."

"This lake is off limits, you know that."

"Yes, sir."

"Then I suggest you turn right around and get yourselves home."

I threw a nervous look back up the path. "But what about the ghost?" I asked.

"Ghost?" he yelled. "Don't tell me you believe those silly rumors."

I swallowed hard and continued to stare up the path. "I don't believe them sir, but I think the ghost might."

"Don't be ridiculous," Mr. Snavely growled. "Now you kids get on home before I call the Sheriff and have you arrested for trespassing."

"Yes, sir."

We glanced at each other. It was a tough decision: stay around and get thrown in jail for trespassing or head back up the trail and run into Casper with the glowing hair.

But since we could no longer hear the ghost, we reluctantly decided to take our chances with the path. We turned, then just before we started, I called back up to the levee. "Mr. Snavely?"

"What is it now?"

"Do you need some help up there?"

"Help? Of course not." But even from the distance I could hear him nervously clearing his throat. "Somebody just uh, well, somebody opened one of the valves up here. Not very smart with this contaminated water and the city just below. Anyway, I just uh, well, the only way to close it down was to come up here personally, so here I am. Now run along and remember work starts at 8:30 sharp tomorrow."

"Yes, sir."

We turned toward the path and started the hike back to the main road. But I could tell Mr. Snavely was lying. Whatever he was up to, he was pretty upset that we'd caught him at it. Which, as you can guess, made me even more nervous about showing up for work tomorrow.

But the good news was we still had the ghost. Maybe with some luck, it would be waiting for us on the path. And maybe with even more luck it would tear me limb from limb so I wouldn't have to go to work.

Then again, we all know about my luck. . . .

Chapter 4

Here We Go Again

"Mr. Snavely? Hello. Mr. Snavely?"

It was 8:30 in the morning when I entered the Water Management Facility.

This was the last place in the world I wanted to be . . . so, of course, it was the only place I could be.

I tried believing what Mom had said about God being in charge of everything and that we should trust Him and "bloom where we're planted." But that stuff is kind of hard to remember when you're busy stepping into your own custom-designed nightmare.

The phone call I'd overheard yesterday was still rattling in my head: *"If that stupid kid is here, I have the perfect alibi—everyone will believe it's his fault."*

"Mr. Snavely?"

Still no answer.

I entered the room with the monitors. The lights were on, the screens were going, and all the gauges were working. But for some reason no one was home.

"Hello?"

I crossed over into the office. Yesterday's disaster had been cleaned up, but there was still no one around. And then I saw it: a note on Mr. Snavely's desk. It had my name scrawled across the top. I moved around the desk and gave it a read.

Wallace,
Have the flu. Had to go home. You're in charge.
Don't worry, everything is automated. Don't do a
thing, and you'll be fine.

Mr. Snavely

WHAT? Leaving me in charge?! Was he out of his mind?! Didn't he know my reputation??

I leaned on the desk trying to steady myself. I looked down at the note again. *Don't do a thing, and you'll be fine.* Well, okay, maybe I could do that. Just as long as I didn't touch anything important . . . or move . . . or breathe.

Slowly I turned and, ever so cautiously, headed back into the room full of monitors.

So far, so good. No major disasters, no Water Management Facility meltdowns.

I crossed to the desk that overlooked the monitors. Then I carefully pulled out the chair and took a seat.

Still no catastrophes. Wow, I was setting some sort of record here. Who knows, maybe I was starting a brand-new trend. Of course I knew better than that. After all, I did have my reputation to keep up. Major destruction was on its way, it was just a matter of whether it was coming before or after lunch.

With nothing to do but hang around and wait for doomsday, I thought I'd pass some time by pulling out ol' Betsy and getting back to my superhero story:

When we last left Tidy Guy, he was zipping toward Planet Getalife, which is being held hostage by the ever-so-sinister and notorious non-tooth flosser...Chaos Kid.

As our hero arrives, he lets out a ghastly gasp. It's worse than expected:

—Cars are no longer staying in their lanes.
—Preschoolers are connecting their dot-to-dot pictures in any order they want.

—Baseball runners are having to
search all over the stadium for
the next base.

Still, it's been a long, hot jour-
ney, and Tidy Guy must chill down with
a little Baskin-Robbins break. As
his spacecraft settles into the parking lot, crushing only a handful of
cars along the way, he sees that
everyone is fighting, yelling, and
screaming. There's so much mayhem that
he thinks he's landed in the middle of
an MTV awards show until he sees there
are no cameras, or screaming cra-
zies, or people running around with
major body parts pierced.

He climbs out of his ship and fights
his way toward the store. Once inside,
he is amazed that everywhere he looks
there is nothing but, you guessed
it...CHAOS. He spots a customer shouting at the clerk behind the counter,
"Chocolate I the Whammie Surprise
thought was the month of flavor!"

Once again our neat freak turns on
his Acme Unscrambler and listens for
the translation:

"I thought Chocolate Whammie Surprise was the flavor of the month!"

"That was back when we had months," the clerk explains.

"Wait your turn," someone screams. "My number is next."

"Not anymore! Now any number follows any other!"

All this over elevator music with no melody and nonsense lyrics. (Hm, maybe he is at that awards show after all.)

Such disorganization is more than our hero can stand. If this is what's happening in public, he can only imagine what's going on in homes: people squeezing toothpaste tubes in the middle, toilet lids being left up, and worst of all worsts—family members not turning their socks right side out before throwing them into the dirty clothes.

But before Tidy Guy gets his underwear in a bunch, an unbearable pain shoots through his jaw. He grabs his mouth and screams: "AUGH! What's happening? What's going on?"

"It's Chaos Kid!" a woman wearing a skirt over her head and a blouse

around her legs cries. She points at
his mouth with the Reebok high-tops
she is wearing for gloves. "He's re-
arranging your mouth. He's mixing up
your teeth."

"No way!" Tidy Guy cries. "After
all the dough my folks dished out for
braces?"

"He's disorganizing everything!" she
screams. "Even our schools. Teachers
are teaching our kids their ABQs, geography professors insist Portland is the
capital of Guatemala, and——"

"What's that?" our hero interrupts,
pointing to a giant luxury liner heading the wrong way down the freeway.

"That's him!" a man cries through the
open fly of the Levis covering his face.
"That's Chaos Kid's headquarters."

Quicker than you can say, "Isn't this
just a little much, even for a McDoogle
story?" Tidy Guy hops back into his
starcruiser and roars off toward Chaos
Kid.

But the closer he roars, the more dis-
organized he becomes. Soon his shirt-
tail comes untucked, next the creases
in his superhero tights disappear,

and worst of all worsts—his hair actually starts to get mussed.

Oh no! Who knows what awful anguish awaits our acne-free hero, what terribly untidy traumas are in store?

And then, suddenly—

BZZZZZZZZZZ.

I leaped higher than a pole-vaulter with hiccups. After crawling back into my skin and restarting my heart, I realized that some sort of alarm was going off in the Water Management Facility.

I scanned the room. Everything looked normal. Everything, that is, but the red alarm flashing under one of the monitors.

I raced to the wall of TV screens for a better look.

I wished I hadn't.

It was the Knox Lake monitor. Actually, it was the gauge under the monitor. The one that read "Lake Capacity." The one where the needle had just dropped below 78 percent.

Now I'm no math whiz, but since all of the other lakes and reservoirs registered 100 percent, I figured we might just have a little problem. And when I glanced up at the screen showing Knox Lake, I realized we had a very major problem.

The water level had dropped a whole lot since last night.

Someone was draining the lake!

Not only that, but if what Mr. Snavely had said was true, then the toxins that were dumping out of that lake were heading straight toward our city!

I had to do something. But after five minutes of yelling for help and throwing myself down on the floor for a good cry, I realized I might want to try another plan. Unfortunately, no other plan came to mind . . . except one.

I remembered Mr. Snavely had said the only way to shut off those valves was to go up there on a motorbike and do it in person.

Wonderful . . . me on a motorbike, all alone at Knox Lake. I could hardly wait. Then again, I guess I really wouldn't be alone. After all, there was still that ghost and still that monster and still who knows what else waiting up there for me. By the looks of things, I guessed I'd be having plenty of company.

And for once in my life, I'd guessed right.

Chapter 5

Ghost Bustin'

Anybody can drive a motorbike, right? Just hop on board and fire up the puppy. I'd seen it done a million times on TV, so no sweat.

Not exactly . . .

First there was the problem of getting it started. I hopped onto the bike and tromped down on the foot lever just like a pro. Except a pro would probably not have chosen the wrong foot lever on the wrong side of the bike, which managed to send the whole thing crashing onto the ground.

The good news was the bike didn't get a single dent. The bad news was it was because my leg cushioned its fall.

"YEOW!"

Once I got the bike back up, I switched to the other foot lever on the other side. I started jumping down on it again and again, and again some more. After about five and a half hours of this incredible fun, I noticed the ignition key.

My, what a novel idea. I reached over, turned the key, and

VAROOOM!

All right!

Next came the problem of finding the gas. I looked all over the bike but couldn't find the gas pedal anywhere. In frustration, I grabbed the handlebar grips and threw my leg over the side to get off. One grip twisted in my hand and the bike shot forward.

I was grateful to have found the gas. I would have been more grateful if I had been sitting on the seat at the time. We zipped out of the parking lot and up the dirt road like a bolt of lightning. Well, the bike did the zipping. I was doing the screaming and the fighting to get back on.

Things might have been a little easier if I wasn't also doing the world's longest wheelie. It seems the more I struggled to crawl back onto the bike, the more I twisted the accelerator grip, and the longer my fantastic stunt continued.

Yes sir, it was quite a sight. And just about the time I thought I should be contacting Barnum and Bailey about a job in the circus, I managed to crawl back into the seat and the bike finally dropped down onto both wheels.

After a while I started to get the hang of the bike. *Hm,* I thought, *if the gas was in the hand grip, then that must mean these little silver things are the brakes.* I gave one a tight squeeze just to make sure I was right, and . . .

SCREECH!

The front wheel suddenly stopped. Unfortunately, the rest of the bike didn't. Neither did its driver. I shot over the top of the handlebars like a human cannonball,

"WOAHHHhhh . . ."

and sailed through the air, head over heels, until I hit a road sign.

KER-SPLAT!

As I carefully peeled my face off the sign, I couldn't help noticing it read:

KNOX LAKE
2 MILES

Or, if you happen to be reading the impression on my face:

+-------------------+
| KNOX LAKE |
| 2 MILES |
+-------------------+

What a comfort to know I was heading in the right direction.

I staggered back to the bike, lifted it up, and resumed my little adventure. If I was having such a great time getting there, I couldn't imagine what fun and games awaited me when I arrived.

I didn't have to wait long. In a matter of minutes the lake came into view. But it wasn't the lake that got my attention. It was the glowing form with the blazing hair moving across the road in front of me. The glowing form with blazing hair that I was about to have a major head-on with!

After letting out the necessary screams of horror, I reached over and squeezed the hand brake for the back wheel. Once again the bike skidded to a stop—this time without all that bothersome end-over-end flipping. Instead, the back end started sliding around.

Oh no, I was losing control! (What a surprise!) A second later I'd dumped the bike onto my good leg—well it had been my good leg. Once again I began doing my bouncing and tumbling routine:

"Ouch! Ouch! Oooow! Boy does that smart!"

Finally I rolled to a stop.

I don't remember much after that, except the crunch of gravel as Mr. Glow-in-the-Dark approached, hovered over me, and finally reached his gnarly claws down to me. Unfortunately, as much as I wanted to stick around and see exactly how my life was going to end, I had more pressing matters to attend to . . . like passing out from total fear.

* * * * *

I must say, heaven was a bit of a disappointment. No music, no clouds, just the worn sofa I was lying on, a cool washcloth covering my forehead, and a little trailer home. What a let-down. I mean, here I had gone to all the trouble of dying, and this was the best God could come up with?

"Are you okay?"

I turned in the direction of the voice and saw the ghost sitting in a chair beside me. Well, it *had* been the ghost. Indoors and closer up, it looked a lot more human. The glow around its body was gone, and its hair now looked more on the pale-gray side than the eerie, glow-in-the-dark variety. Oh, and one other thing. At this range it no longer looked like an it; it looked more like a she.

"Are you okay?" she repeated.

I moved slightly and winced at the wrecking ball slamming around inside my head.

"Easy now," she said. "You've had a nasty spill; you better rest quietly a few more minutes."

"Wh-where am I?" I stuttered. "And who-who . . ." I swallowed and tried again, "Who-who-who—"

I guess she was getting tired of my owl impersonation and gave me a hand. "Who am I?" she asked.

I nodded, grateful for the help.

"My name is Dr. Ventura."

"A doctor?" I croaked. "You were a doctor before you . . . you know . . . before you died?"

"Died?" she asked. "I haven't died."

"But how can you be a ghost if you haven't died?"

She broke into gentle laughter and tossed her long, frizzy hair to the side. "Gracious me, I'm no ghost."

"You're not?"

"Of course not. Though I must say those rumors have certainly allowed me to continue my work in relative obscurity."

"Relative what?"

"I've been able to continue my studies without too many curiosity seekers getting in the way. Though between this morning and last night, I've certainly had my share of visitors lately."

My heart started pounding a little faster. "That was you last night?" I asked. "Up on the path, in the woods?"

She smiled. "So we've met before."

I nodded.

"Well, I must say you look a little different with your pants on."

I could feel my face heat up with embarrassment. "But last night . . . " I said. "Last night you were all glowing . . . and your hair was all white . . . and, I mean, you were lit up like a ghost."

She touched her hair and answered, "My hair's been white like this for years. Some people say it's my finest feature."

"Well sure, I mean it's beautiful, but what about—"

She nodded across the room. On the peg next to the door was a pair of aluminum overalls. And beside them, metallic gloves. "I wear those whenever I go down to the lake," she said. "The worst toxins have been cleaned up since Iatds started roaming the bottom, but those clothes are still a good precaution."

I'd barely heard the last part of the sentence. It was the phrase *Iatds started roaming the bottom* that caught my attention. So there *was* something living in the lake. The mystery about the ghost may have been cleared up (though I still planned to keep my eye on her just in case she started floating around and passing through walls and stuff), but not the mystery of the monster. It was real. Not only did she know about it, but she had actually given it a name.

"Why are you up here?" she asked.

I started doing the usual blah-blah about Career Days and how I was assigned to the Water Management Facility and how I hated it and how Mom said to "bloom where I was planted." The doc pretended to be interested, but when I finally got around to the gauges showing a major drop in the water level, her attention really picked up.

"I thought there was a problem," she said, rising to her feet and beginning to pace. "That means someone is draining the lake."

"They can't do that," I said.

"Why not?" she asked.

"If they drain the lake, isn't that going to pollute the reservoirs downstream? Won't that contaminate Middletown's drinking water?"

She nodded and looked even more worried. "Yes, whoever is doing this must have some very strong reasons." She crossed to the phone. "We need to warn the authorities before the water gets too far into the system, before the townspeople start drinking it."

She raised the phone to her ear but was stopped by a loud thumping. At first I thought it was my heart doing its usual cardiac arrest bit (after all, meeting ghosts, chatting about their pet monsters, and realizing your entire town is about to be poisoned isn't the most relaxing way to spend your day). But when the doc crossed to the window to look outside, I realized it must be something else.

She parted the curtains just in time for us to watch a helicopter touch down between the lake and the trailer. It was less than a hundred yards away. I staggered to my feet for a better look. That would have been easier if I hadn't been lying on one leg and if that one leg hadn't fallen asleep. But after a couple of trips and stumbles along the way, I finally joined the doctor.

The helicopter looked pretty cool . . . except for the two men in suits and sunglasses who were climbing out. The first one, the passenger, was so tall he could have played for the Sonics. The second one, the pilot, was so short I doubted he'd ever be able to get on any of the roller coasters with those "You Must Be This Tall" signs.

But their height wasn't the uncool part. The

uncool part was the automatic rifles they slung over their shoulders. Even that wouldn't have been so bad except for their turning and spotting us at the window and then racing toward us for all they were worth.

That was uncool. Way uncool.

Chapter 6

A Little Hide-and-Seek

Doc quickly pulled back from the window. "Come on," she ordered. "We've got to get out of here."

"What about warning the officials about the lake?"

"That'll have to wait." She grabbed a set of car keys from the table and reached for a little portable radio device. "If we don't get out of here, there'll be nobody around to warn them." She turned and headed for the back door.

"What's going on?" I asked. "Who are those guys?"

"I'll explain later. Just follow me."

Now the way I figured it, I had two choices: follow this woman who still might be haunting houses in her spare time, or stick around and chat with the rifle-toting suits. Who knows, maybe those guys weren't so bad after all. Maybe they just came up here to do a little target practice. Then again, by the way they were racing toward us, it looked like they'd already picked out *who* their targets would be.

We arrived at the back door and Doc cautiously opened it. Her beat-up van was about fifty feet away. She moved down the steps and motioned for me to silently follow.

I obeyed . . . well, except for the silently part. It seems my left foot still hadn't entirely woken up from its little nap. The first step went fine. It was the second one that got me. After that, everything went downhill . . . literally.

"WOAHhhh"—*BANG, CRASH, CLANG!*

The *WOAHhhh* was me crying out as I fell. The *Bang, Crash, Clang!* was me bouncing down the steps face first.

"They're around back!" I heard one of the men shout. "Around back!"

Doc stooped to help me, but by the time she pulled me to my feet, we could hear them running around the corner. They were practically on top of us.

"Under here," she whispered as she grabbed me and shoved me beneath the trailer. "Hurry."

I scrambled through the dead leaves and the

slimy who-knows-whats. Doc was right behind. We'd barely settled in before the first pair of feet raced passed. And that's all we could see: feet. The guy was so tall we couldn't see past his ankles. A moment later, he was joined by his partner, who was so short we not only saw his feet, but also his legs, his stomach, and his chest.

"I don't, uh, get it," the tall one said, sounding a little short on brain cells. "She, was, uh, right here. I'm sure I heard her."

"She couldn't have gotten far," Short Suit said. "Go and check out the van. Disable it if you have to. I'll go inside the trailer and secure the place. Maybe she left the remote behind. That'll make our job a lot easier."

"Uh, sure thing, Boss." Tall Suit headed out toward the van as Short Suit turned and climbed up the steps into the trailer.

Now, I'd be lying if I said it wasn't gross being sprawled out under the trailer in all that slime and stuff. I mean, who knew what type of creepy crawlies were starting to slither over our bodies?

"Don't worry," Doc whispered. "We're safe here."

I nodded, thinking this was obviously a new definition of the word *safe*. Already I could feel my legs itching with all sorts of imagined things crawling on them. Of course I knew it was just my imagination, but still . . .

I tried to take my mind off it by leaning over and asking her, "What's going on? What do those guys want?"

She motioned to the radio control thingie she had scooped off the table.

"What is that?" I whispered.

"It's Iatds's controls."

"You can control the monster?"

"If I invented it, I ought to be able to control it."

"You invented it?"

"Of course. The Independent Analyzer and Toxin Disposal System has always been my brainchild."

"The what?"

"The I.A.T.D.S. I've been developing it here with a government grant for months."

"You mean it's not a monster?"

"Hardly," she whispered. "Iatds's sole purpose is to go in and clean up toxic spills."

My frown deepened.

She continued. "It's like an automatic pool cleaner but much more advanced. I still have a few kinks to work out, but eventually Iatds will be able to patrol any body of water and clean and purify it independent of any human assistance."

"So that's what I saw on the monitor?" I whispered. "Just a fancy underwater robot?"

"If you're talking about the monitor at the Water Management Facility," she answered, "yes."

Although this was all pretty interesting, it still wasn't enough to stop my imagination about all the crawlies. Not only did I imagine they were swarming over my legs, but now I actually thought they were crawling around my waist. "Who are these guys?" I whispered. "Why do they want you?"

"They're from Ecodyne; it's a huge, international corporation. They don't want me, they want Iatds. He can make them millions. They've made offers to buy him, but I won't sell, not yet. Not until I get the kinks worked out." She let out a quiet sigh. "But now it looks like they've stopped offering and are going to start taking."

"What type of kinks do you have to work out?" I asked.

"Sometimes Iatds can't tell the difference between pollution and life forms."

"Life forms?" I asked, scratching and rubbing around my waist.

"Yeah, like fish, animals . . . sometimes even human swimmers."

"That could be a problem," I agreed. But the conversation was doing no good. I still couldn't take my mind off the itching and crawling. In fact, it was worse than ever. I was even imagining them on my back and chest.

"Wait a minute," she suddenly said. "Now I understand."

"What?"

"These guys are the ones draining the lake. Of course. They're planing to go out onto the dry lake bed and just scoop up Iatds."

"What about the town?" I whispered, continuing to scratch my imaginary buddies.

"We're talking millions, maybe billions of dollars. They don't care about poisoning one little town. In fact, they could—" She finally noticed my scratching and came to a stop. "Are you okay?"

"Yeah," I shrugged. "It's just my imagination. I keep thinking there are bugs under here and that they're crawling all over me. In fact, right now, I actually think I feel them moving on my arms. Stupid, huh?" I held out an arm to her. "But as you can see, there's nothing here but . . ." It was then that I noticed my arm was swarming with movement. "Nothing but a billion beetles . . . a billion beetles all crawling *ALL OVER ME!!*"

I kinda forgot to whisper that last part. Actually, I kinda yelled it at the top of my lungs.

I guess you could say our cover was blown. We scurried out of there just as Tall Suit spun around from the van, spotted us, and began pursuit. We could also hear Short Suit running inside the trailer, anxious to join our little party.

"Run," Doc shouted. "Run!"

I didn't have to be told twice. Between the

swarming beetles and the guys with guns, the last thing in the world I wanted was to stand still.

In a matter of seconds, Doc and I hit the woods, flying like the wind . . . which, unfortunately, is not quite as fast as flying like a bullet.

Crack, *zing*
Crack, *zing*

"They're shooting at us!" I cried.

"Don't worry," she shouted. "They're just trying to scare us!"

Suddenly the limb above my head exploded into a thousand splinters.

"They're doing a pretty good job!" I yelled.

"Keep running!"

I tell you, for being an old-timer (she was way over thirty), Doc was in pretty good shape. And for being the world's worst athlete, I did a pretty good job at keeping up. True, I would have done a better job if I weren't busy swatting beetles and tearing off my clothes to get rid of them. But, other than that, everything was going fine . . . until I got my T-shirt stuck. I can't exactly explain it, but there's something about running through the woods while getting your T-shirt caught over your head that can create a few problems.

BAM—"OW!"

I don't want to say that the trees were hard . . .

BAM—"OW!"
BAM—"OW!"

Or that doing my imitation of a human pinball bouncing off them wasn't fun . . .

BAM—"OW!"
BAM—"OW!"
BAM—"OW!"

But a guy can only take so many concussions before he starts to get a little bored with all the pain.

Fortunately, Doc came to my rescue and ripped the T-shirt the rest of the way off. Unfortunately, it felt like she also ripped off most of my ears. When I finally saw daylight, I noticed we had doubled back and were heading past the trailer toward the lake.

"What are you doing?" I shouted.

She motioned me to be quiet. "While they're

chasing us in the woods, we can make a getaway."
She pointed toward a small rowboat. "That's my
dinghy over there. We can cross the lake and get
help."

It was a great plan (even though I get seasick
just taking a bath). When we arrived I quickly
climbed into the boat.

"What's that?" she whispered.

I turned to see Doc squinting at the lake. I followed her vision and saw a pretty good-sized
motorboat quickly approaching.

"All right!" I cried. "We've got help."

Doc threw a look back into the woods, then
turned toward the motorboat. She began waving
her arms to get its attention.

It spotted us and picked up speed. At first I
didn't recognize the driver, but the closer he got,
the more familiar he looked.

"Mr. Snavely!" I shouted. "Mr. Snavely!"

"Wallace?" he cried. "Is that you?"

I gave a huge nod as he cut the engine and
coasted toward shore. "Boy, am I glad you're here,"
I said. "Listen, we gotta go. Some men came in that
helicopter over there and they're trying to steal a
monster from Doc, who I thought was a ghost
but isn't 'cause she invented the monster, which
actually isn't a monster and somebody's threatening the city's water supply by draining . . ."

I stopped jabbering for two reasons. First, there's this thing I have about breathing. And second, I noticed Mr. Snavely wasn't listening. Instead, he was just looking at Doc.

"How have you been, Sarah?" he asked.

"Fine," she said.

"That's great!" I cried, having caught my breath. "So you two know each other. That's swell, but if it's not too much bother, do you think you could get reacquainted a little later so we can get out of here before they—"

I was interrupted by the suits' voices. "There they are!"

I spun around just in time to see them emerge from the woods.

"That's them!" I turned back to Mr. Snavely. "That's them! We gotta get outa here!"

But nobody moved.

"Look, I don't want to make a big deal out of this, but those guys with the guns are not good guys. And since I'm kind of allergic to getting shot, I mean I break out in a bad case of death every time it happens, could we please—"

"Wally?" Mr. Snavely interrupted.

"Yes, sir?"

"Shut up."

His rudeness surprised me. But not as much as the next statement. It came from Short Suit as he continued approaching. "Snavely," he shouted, "you've caught them. Excellent."

I spun back to Mr. Snavely. "You know these guys?"

"Know us?" Tall Suit giggled as they finally arrived. "He like works for us, don't he, Boss?"

But Short Suit didn't answer. He was too busy flirting with Doc. "Good afternoon, Dr. Ventura."

Call it a wild guess, but by the daggers shooting out of her eyes, I could tell Doc wasn't especially knocked out about seeing him.

Short Suit's grin faded as quickly as it had appeared. "Get her into the trailer," he ordered. "And take the kid with her."

Chapter 7

All Cooped Up with No Place to Go

Exactly 3.5 minutes later Doc and I found ourselves back in her trailer. The bad guys were doing the usual bad guy things: ripping out her phone, threatening her a lot, and, of course, smoking. They demanded that the Doc use her remote control thingie and call Iatds to the surface. That way they could dismantle him and take the important parts back to their headquarters.

No problem, except for the part where Doc refused.

"Okay, fine," Short Suit sneered. "Then we'll just go ahead and finish draining the lake. By tomorrow morning we'll be able to stroll out onto that lake bed and take it without your help."

"Not only that," Tall Suit said, "but we'll be able to stroll out onto that lake bed and take it without your help."

We all turned to him, amazed at his incredible lack of brain voltage. He smiled, obviously pleased that he had impressed us.

"But what about Middletown?" I protested. "You're going to poison their water."

"Serves them right," Mr. Snavely growled. "For years I've been working at that plant, pouring my heart and soul into it. Never a word of thanks, barely a raise in pay. Nothing but those stupid sewer jokes, that's all I ever got."

Suddenly I remembered. "What about that nice trophy? You know, the one I smashed to smithereens?"

He gave me a look that made me wish my memory hadn't been so good . . . or my mouth so big.

"That's enough small talk," Short Suit snapped. "Lock them in the bathroom, and let's get on with our work."

As they hustled us into the tiny room, I tried to explain that I really didn't have to go to the lavatory and, even if I did, I wouldn't with a lady right there beside me. But they had a lot of other bad-guy stuff on their minds and didn't pay much attention. Soon, the two of us were stashed in a room just a little smaller than a box of Milk Duds.

"Great," I sighed as I plopped myself down on the edge of the toilet seat. "This is just great."

"Relax," Doc said. She was already searching

the room. "There's got to be a way we can use this to our advantage."

I couldn't help rolling my eyes. "You sound just like my mom."

"How so?" Doc asked, as she continued her search.

"She keeps telling me to use every situation. To 'bloom where I'm planted,' she says. I don't want to complain, but it doesn't look like we'll be doing a lot of blooming here."

Doc's eyes locked onto the small window in the wall. It was the type with a bunch of narrow glass panes running across it. She crossed to it and immediately began working to slip those panes out of their frames.

"What are you doing?" I whispered.

"Your mother might not be so wrong. Of all the rooms to lock us in, this is the best."

"Really?" I rose to my feet. "What can I do?"

She gave me an aren't-you-the-klutz-that-was-just-banging-around-into-all-those-trees look. "I'm sorry, Wally, but from what I've seen of your coordination, it might be better if you just sit quietly and try not to help."

I nodded, once again amazed at how quickly my reputation spreads.

The minutes dragged on. I wished I'd brought ol' Betsy. Now would be a good time to continue my superhero story. Unfortunately, I'd left my computer back at the Water Management Facility. Still, Doc carried a half dozen pens in her pocket (I think that's part of the uniform for scientists), and there was a nearby roll of toilet paper. So I borrowed a pen, pulled on the roll, and went to work. After all, when a guy's gotta create, he's gotta create. . . .

When we last left our incurably neat and carefully manicured hero, Tidy Guy was approaching a giant cruise ship heading the wrong way down the freeway. A cruise ship that is none other than Chaos Kid's headquarters.

But the closer Tidy Guy approaches the cruise ship, the more chaos he experiences. It is even affecting his spaceship. The gas pedal has already traded places with his door handle. To use his rearview mirror he must now crawl into the glove compartment.

And worst of all worsts . . . when he drops in his latest D.C. Talk cassette, he winds up hearing "Sesame Street's Greatest Hits"!

Then, just when he's about to lose his mind (you try listening to "The Alphabet Song" a hundred times), he finally gets his craft landed. But when he pulls on the door handle, he suddenly shoots back into the sky. (Stupid gas pedal, anyway.)

Having to use the cigarette lighter as a steering wheel, he eventually touches down again. And, after crawling out of the gas tank (now the exit hatch), he finds himself standing beside a giant and notorious generator that is blasting out the even gianter and notoriouser Chaos Beam.

And, directly in front of that generator is the corruptibly crummy and incorrigibly cross

(insert bad guy music here)
Chaos Kid.

No one's sure what made Chaos
Kid so chaotic. Some say it was
his mom forcing him to make his
bed one too many times. Others
say he spent too many hours
staring at those squiggly patterns
trying to find a 3-D picture.
Then there's the ever-popular
theory that he actually tried to
make sense out of all the buttons
on his VCR remote.

Whatever the reason, Chaos Kid
is dysfunctional in a major if-I-
can't-rule-the-universe-then-I-
at-least-want-to-destroy-it
kind of way.

"So, Guy Tidy . . ." he sneers a
sinister sneer, "meet again, we."

Tidy Guy reaches for his Acme
Unscrambler and cranks it all
the way to Ultra-Mess. But he is
too close to the beam; its power is
just too strong.

*"up Give it," Chaos Kid grins.
"over all It is."*

*Tidy Guy fights the panic
rising inside and cries, "me don't
You scare!"*

*His eyes widen in horror. Scott
Great, he thinks, my speaking it
even affecting is! And then, only
that not, but my thinking
affecting it is, too!*

*Desperately he tries to figure
out a solution. do What do I? do
What do I? And then, just when
his thoughts are more scrambled
than a three-egg omelet—*

I'd reached the end of the toilet paper. Great, it
was just like my house, an almost empty roll that
nobody had bothered to replace. But before I could
get too worked up, Doc motioned me toward the
window. All the panes had been removed and it
was wide open. "I'll boost you through," she
said, "then I'll follow."

I let her boost me up, and with the usual daily
requirement of McDoogle klutziness, I finally

made it through the window and dropped to the ground outside. Unfortunately, the ground outside was home to a bunch of garbage cans

*BANG CLATTER CLATTER
RATTLE BANG BANG!*

The back door to the trailer flew open, and I froze.

"Who's there?" It was Short Suit.

I thought of answering him, but since I have this thing called a brain, I decided to stay silent.

He started down the steps, and I flattened down into a pile of garbage that smelled like my gym socks after one too many months of nonstop wearing.

"It's just the raccoons," Mr. Snavely's voice called from inside the trailer. "They start coming out at the end of the day. Don't be so jumpy."

For a second there was no movement. I could tell Short Suit was not entirely buying the raccoon bit. It could go either way. He could head back into the house or come out and see me doing a very bad imitation of a Hefty Trash bag. But after a ton of prayers, including promises to never again sneak soda pop out of the refrigerator (let alone fill the container back up with water—poor Mom could never figure out why the pop was always so flat), I finally heard the footsteps turn and head back up the steps.

With a sigh of relief and a reminder to God that I hadn't said anything about chocolate milk and all the other cool stuff in the fridge (though I suspected He wouldn't let me get away with that kind of fine print), I whispered up to Doc, "It's all clear."

She effortlessly crawled through the window and dropped to my side.

"Sorry about all the noise," I whispered.

"Don't worry about it," she said. "In fact, you've given me an idea. Let's get the garbage back in one of the cans and take it with us."

"What?"

"You'll see. Hurry."

I followed her orders. After quietly loading up a can, we each took a side handle and ran toward the lake with the can between us.

"Look at the water," I whispered. "It's still going down."

"Yes, we've got to hurry."

The sun was just setting as we got to the lake and silently loaded the garbage can onto the rowboat. Well, at least that's what we wanted to do. But since this took some coordination, I ended up banging the can into the side of the boat half a dozen times and falling into the water. Unfortunately, my little dip wasn't all that refreshing, and by the way the slimy water clung to me, I could see that the lake wasn't completely cleaned up.

Then, before I could really enjoy the toxins, the front door to the trailer flew open and I heard our buddies shouting, "There they are! They're getting away!"

"Quick!" Doc shouted. "Push off, Wally! Push off!"

I did my best, but not without taking another dip in the lake along the way. By the time I dragged myself into the boat, I could hear their footsteps crunching on the sand right behind us.

"Row, Wally, row!"

I grabbed an oar and began rowing for all I was worth.

Meanwhile, the bad guys were doing the usual bad-guy yelling and swearing (I'd type out the words, but I'm trying to keep my fingers "G" rated). Anyway, the three of them clamored into their boat, cranked up the engine, and started after us.

It didn't seem fair, a major powerboat against a little rowboat, especially since I was helping to row (which basically meant we were going around in circles). The good news was they'd forgotten to bring their guns. The bad news was this didn't stop them from ramming into us and trying to sink us.

K-BAM!

"Augh!" we cried.

"Go back to shore!" they shouted. "Go back to shore or we'll sink you!"

K-BAM!

Doc spun around to me and yelled, "Grab the garbage can!"

"What?"

"Grab the garbage can and start dumping it into the water!"

I wanted to argue, but Doc looked pretty determined, so I followed her orders. Milk cartons, leftover coffee grounds, you name it, I dumped it. Of course I felt a little bad about littering (and seeing those returnable pop bottles float away), but it's hard to be too ecologically minded when you're busy being killed.

K-BAM!

The bad guys rammed our boat again.

Then the weirdest thing happened. I noticed the water around us was starting to move and swirl.

"What's that?" I shouted.

"Just keep dumping!" Doc shouted. "Keep dumping!"

I did. And the more I dumped, the more the water turned and churned.

"What's going on?" Short Suit shouted. The water had gone from churning to bubbling and boiling. "What are you doing?"

But Doc didn't answer. She was too busy staring at her watch, counting down the seconds.

Water splashed everywhere.

"What's happening?" I cried.

"Just a few more seconds!" Doc shouted. "Hang on!"

I grabbed the sides of the boat. Things were starting to go crazy, out of control. It was like floating inside a giant teapot that was boiling on high.

And then Doc screamed. "Now! Row, Wally! Row like you've never rowed before!"

Chapter 8

Up, Up, and Not Quite Away

Our little rowboat was rocking and rolling in a major sort of way. There were times I couldn't even tell where the water began and the boat ended. But that didn't stop me from following Doc's orders.

I was rowing, big time. And for once in my life, I was almost doing it right.

We'd only gone a few yards before I heard this terrible cracking and splintering sound followed by shouts and screams. I started to turn, but Doc yelled, "Don't look back! Keep rowing!"

Still, I had to see. I had to know what was happening to the bad guys. I spun around for just a second. Through the splashing and spraying water, I saw their entire boat rising into the air. It was incredible. The middle was splitting in two as the men screamed for their lives. And for good reason.

Directly below them was what looked like part sea monster, part machine. Its giant black head continued to rise and push the boat high into the air, while its long, slithering tentacles whipped in all directions, grabbing floating garbage and cramming it into its monstrous mouth.

"HELP US!" the men in the motorboat screamed. *"HELP US!"*

"Keep rowing, Wally. Keep rowing and don't look back!"

Now I understood. All the garbage had summoned Doc's Iatds to the surface.

The screams grew more terrifying and were followed by a powerful *CRASH!*

And suddenly there was nothing. Only eerie silence. The water was still spraying and splashing, but the screaming had mysteriously stopped.

I wanted to turn back, to try and help, but I knew if we didn't get out of there, we'd be next on the monster's menu. Doc and I kept rowing, straining against the oars for all we were worth, when suddenly—

SCRAPE!

We'd hit the beach.

"Hurry!" Doc grabbed my shoulder, half guiding, half shoving me out of the boat. But I had to see. I had to take one last look.

The water was already settling down, but the boat was nowhere to be seen. There were no boards, no splinters, nothing. Iatds had done his job well, too well.

The only thing he'd missed were the Two Suits and Mr. Snavely, who suddenly bobbed to the surface, coughing and cursing and thrashing in the water.

I turned to Doc. She was looking at the trailer, searching for a getaway. The van had already been trashed, and the telephone had been ripped out. Of course we could do the run-in-the-woods routine, but that hadn't been too successful the last time. With the lake draining so quickly, we had another problem. Not only did we need to get away from the bad guys, but we had to warn the people in town.

"Let's go!" Doc grabbed my hand and dragged me toward the helicopter.

"You know how to fly that?" I shouted.

"It's been a long time," she yelled as we ran toward it.

Behind us, I could hear the bad guys already on their feet, sloshing toward shore. When they saw where we were heading they started yelling, but neither of us wanted to hang around and chat. We arrived at the helicopter and Doc threw open the door. "Get in, get in!" she shouted.

I crawled over the pilot's seat and toward mine.

Well, at least I tried to crawl toward mine. It seems my feet got a little tangled up in a bunch of foot levers and stuff.

"Quit fooling around, Wally!"

I hadn't the heart to explain that this was me functioning at peak performance. Fortunately, after a lot more squirming and kicking (which unfortunately meant hitting a lot of switches and buttons on the control panel) I finally managed to tumble into my seat.

Doc was right behind me. "Buckle up!" she cried. "Buckle up and put on that hard hat on the floor."

I spotted the hat. The back read Ecodyne, Inc. It was obviously something from the bad guys' home office.

"Why the hard hat?" I shouted.

"Like I said, it's been a long time."

I slipped on the hat, wondering how a protected head would stop the rest of my body from being folded, stapled, and mutilated in a crash. But I knew better than to ask. Doc was already firing up the giant overhead rotor.

Things were going to be close. The guys were out of the water and staggering toward us. It was then I noticed the weirdest thing. For some reason, giant strips of their clothing were missing.

"What's with their clothes?" I shouted over the whining rotor. "What happened to their clothes?"

"They got lucky."

Obviously this was a new definition of the term *lucky*. "What do you mean?" I shouted.

"Iatds's problem is that he can't always distinguish between living and nonliving material."

"What's that got to do with—"

"Their clothes are not living," Doc almost laughed. "This time Iatds only went for their clothes, not their bodies. Next time they might not be so lucky."

The whine of the rotor had grown to a roar. Any second we'd be airborne. Doc used one hand to buckle herself in while pulling back on the stick between us with the other. "Hang on, here we go."

The roar increased. The helicopter started to rise. We were almost out of there. But suddenly we came crashing back to the ground. Doc's door flew open and Mr. Snavely's hand appeared. Doc let out a scream as he grabbed her arm. She tried to slam the door on him, but he was holding on too tight.

She kept pulling on the stick with her right hand while trying to push Mr. Snavely away with her left. I reached over to try and help, but she shouted, "No Wally! The stick. Grab the stick!"

"What?!"

"Grab the stick and pull!" she shouted. "Pull us up. Pull us up!"

I tried grabbing the stick with my right hand and helping her with my left. But it was no good. The engine strained louder under the extra weight as Mr. Snavely hung on like a bulldog. If it weren't for the Doc's seat belt, he would have completely pulled her out.

Suddenly there was noise on my side. I spun around to see Short Suit throwing open *my* door.

"Pull!" Doc screamed. "Pull the stick harder! Pull it!"

Short Suit reached for me.

"Pull it!"

I pulled on the stick with both hands. The chopper started to rise. Short Suit grabbed my arm but was unable to hang on. As we rose, he slipped away—not, of course, without your standard bad-guy rantings and swearing.

But not Mr. Snavely. As my side rose, he kept hanging on to Doc, so that the extra weight kept their side down. We were going to tip over; we were going to crash. The rotor was going to smash into the ground sending pieces of it in a zillion directions.

I started to let go, to reach over and help Doc, but she cried, "Keep pulling! Keep pulling!"

"We're going to crash!" I yelled. "He's pulling us ove—"

Before I could finish, Doc reached for her seat harness and unsnapped it. With nothing to hold her in, Mr. Snavely's weight pulled her out of the cockpit, and they both went tumbling to the ground. The weight loss immediately made the helicopter shoot into the air faster than a cork underwater.

I was airborne. Big time.

That was the good news. The bad news was I didn't know beans about flying a helicopter!

Chapter 9

A Little Night Swim

Flying a helicopter is a lot like flying one of those video games . . . except for all the pedals, dials, and millions of instruments you can't keep track of. Then, of course there's the smashing of your body as it gets thrown all around the cockpit because you don't have a clue what you're doing. And let's not forget the money. Video arcades give you three crashes for a quarter.

Helicopters can kill you once for free.

"Ohhh . . .
      Ahhh . . .
            Eeee . . .
                  Owww . . ."

I was going nowhere fast. Actually, I was going everywhere at the same time. Up, down, sideways.

You name it, I was there, with my stomach and the rest of my insides trying to catch up (or throw up). Then, just to break the monotony (life-threatening horror can get so boring sometimes), I suddenly found myself doing some fancy aerobatics.

Like flying upside down!

It was about then that I learned something very important about helicopters . . .

They don't fly upside down!

"AUGHHHHHHHHHHH . . . "

It's a strange feeling to look above your head and see the earth racing toward you at a billion miles an hour. It's even stranger to realize you're on your way to meet God without getting a chance to change into some decent clothes. Luckily, by the way Knox Lake was rushing at me, I'd at least get the chance to bathe.

KER-SPLAT!
RRrrrrrRRrrrrrRRrrrrrRRrrr

The *KER-SPLAT* was the helicopter hitting the water. The *RRrrrrrRRrrrrrRRRrrrr* was the rotor doing a very bad imitation of an eggbeater. But before it could really work the lake into a froth, there was one final sound—

GLUG-GLUG-GLUG-GLUG . . .

That's right, the cockpit was filling up faster than my handkerchief on a bad allergy day. Part of me wanted to be the good captain and go down with my ship, but because I never quite mastered the art of breathing water, I decided to get out of there as fast as I could.

But I was stuck. Something was holding me down, pressing me into the seat, refusing to let go. And the harder I tried to break away, the stronger its grip grew. The water level rose closer and closer to my head. It was all over.

But as I sat there, wondering who they were going to get to play my part in *Rescue 911,* I glanced down and made a startling discovery. It might be easier to get out if I unfastened my seat harness.

Quicker than you can wonder how anyone with my incredible unintelligence made it as far as the seventh grade (or question the public education system that got me this far), I unsnapped the buckle and kicked my way out of the cockpit.

That was the good news. But, as always, there was some bad news, too.

I had crashed into the part of the lake where I'd first seen Mr. Snavely—near the levee with all of the valves on top of the wall. But it wasn't the valves on top of the wall that worried me. It was the giant drainpipe inside the wall that had my attention—the giant drainpipe that had been opened when Mr. Snavely turned those valves. And that drainpipe was now sucking all the water out of the lake, sending it splashing a hundred feet to the rocks below.

Don't get me wrong. I've got nothing against giant drainpipes sucking water and sending it crashing a hundred feet below. I just wasn't crazy about being part of that water. That's right. As only McDoogle luck would have it, I was smack dab in the middle of a rushing current that was heading even smacker dabber for the giant drainpipe.

I began swimming for all I was worth (which if I didn't hurry, would soon be less than nothing). First I swam to the left.

No good.

Then to the right.

Ditto in the failure department. The current was just too strong.

The pipe was less than 100 feet away. Better make that 90, er 80 . . . uh, well you probably get the idea.

But that was only part of my problem.

Yes sir, what McDoogle catastrophe would be complete without a few other nightmares thrown in just to liven things up? So there I was, minding my own business, just trying to die like any other abnormal human being, when suddenly, a giant tentacle splashed out of the water beside me.

I wanted to scream, but it's hard to scream when you're too scared to breathe. I stared helplessly at the black slithering thing as it continued to splash about, obviously trying to find me. Of course it was my old friend Iatds, the mechanical monster that can't always tell the difference between a living human being and pollution. Apparently, he'd heard all of my thrashing and splashing and figured it was time to come over and clean up the neighborhood.

I looked back to check the distance to the pipe. T-minus-40-feet and counting.

I was all confused. Should I scream my head off because I was about to plummet to my death through an overly thirsty drainpipe or because I was about to be destroyed by some mechanical monster with an eating disorder?

Decisions, decisions, decisions.

Then a second tentacle popped up beside me. Then a third. Now they were all over the place, flying back and forth like bullwhips gone crazy. The black rubbery arms were barely missing me on each pass.

But there was one more element to add to the

nightmare. I managed to catch a glimpse of flashing police lights barreling down the distant road. *Great,* I thought. *This is just perfect. If I don't die as Iatds's late-night snack or by being swept through the pipe, I can always look forward to being arrested for trespassing.*

I wasn't sure if they could arrest me after I was dead, but I was sure they'd at least tell my folks . . . and I knew that would mean getting grounded for life (although that would only be about another 16.3 seconds).

Thinking of my folks made me remember Mom's little sayings. You know, about God causing everything to work together for good and that I should bloom where I am planted. Good ol' Mom. I didn't want to disappoint her, but it looked like the only blooming I'd be doing would involve pushing up daisies at the local cemetery.

I turned toward the pipe. It was seven feet away. Its darkness was already starting to close in around me.

I threw one last look at Iatds. His entire body had surfaced, complete with that monstrous black head and some glowing little eyes. And of course those grotesque arms that continued to flail and flop in all directions.

But it didn't matter. I had entered the pipe.

Yes sir, it had been close, but the pipe had

won. Any second I'd fly out the other end and be smashed to smithereens. It all came to this. My entire life reduced to a giant blob of polluted pond scum sailing out of a pipe and crashing into some very unfriendly (not to mention very unsoft) rocks below.

And then, just as my self-pity was reaching an all-time high, I felt a rubbery arm slither around my shoulders and tighten its embrace. I wanted to tell him it was too late, he'd lost, and besides I didn't believe in going steady, particularly with slithering mechanical monsters. But somehow I figured he'd miss the humor.

Come to think of it, so would I.

I was deep inside the pipe, racing toward the other end, but the tentacle would not let go. In fact, its grip grew even tighter, and it began fighting against the current, gradually slowing me down. In a matter of seconds, I had stopped altogether. Water and slime splashed all over me, but I was going nowhere. Ol' Iatds wasn't letting go.

Then, he actually started pulling me backward *against* the current. Talk about strong. The thing was reeling me upstream, out of the pipe, and back into the lake.

A moment later I saw the sky. Wow, talk about lucky. Things were really looking up. Unfortunately, just a little too "up."

Iatds suddenly lifted me out of the water and raised me high into the air. I knew I was heading toward his mouth, that I was about to become his latest munchie, but I no longer cared. Not because I was brave or fearless or anything like that.

I quit caring because it's tough to care when you've passed out from fear.

Chapter 10

Wrapping Up

I woke up and breathed a sigh of relief. Talk about a nightmare. Can you believe it? I actually dreamed I had crashed into some polluted lake and was being sucked out by a giant drainpipe while being chased by a giant techno-monster. Talk about weird. I tell you, I've really got to do something about my imagination.

At least that's what I thought until I opened my eyes and saw the polluted lake with a giant techno-monster hovering just offshore.

Then I realized I better do something about my life.

"Wally?"

I turned my head to see Mom and Dad looking down at me. Past them were a handful of police cars and an ambulance.

"Are you okay, son?" Dad asked.

"What happened?" I struggled to sit up and saw I was on an ambulance gurney.

"Lie back down and rest," Mom said.

"But you don't understand," I croaked. "They're draining the lake! The bad guys, they talked Mr. Snavely into helping them steal Doc's invention and Middletown's drinking water is going to be—"

"It's all under control, Wally." It was Doc's voice. She came into view, smiling. "When you were climbing into the helicopter and kicking all those switches and everything, you accidentally turned on the radio."

"I did?"

"Middletown Airport heard us, got a fix on us, and contacted the police."

"But the water," I said. "You've got to stop the water from contaminating the other reservoir—"

"That's all taken care of," Dad said. "Officials are warning everyone in town not to drink any tap water until they get the system cleaned up."

"Which should only take a day or two because Iatds has already removed the worst toxins," Doc explained. "After that, everything will be fine."

I felt myself relaxing a little, although I still had about a zillion questions. "How'd I get out?" I asked.

"Iatds saved you."

"He did?"

"It was the most amazing thing." Doc glowed.

"He just picked you right out of the water and plopped you down here on the beach safe and sound."

"Only because you remained cool and calm and had the courage not to panic," Dad said.

I wanted to explain it's hard to have courage when you've fainted, but he looked so pleased I didn't really want to burst his bubble.

"And the best thing," Doc continued, "is that you've put Iatds through an incredible test, and he passed with flying colors."

"I did?"

"Absolutely. Not only was he able to distinguish a human being from pollution, but he was actually able to save your life. You've proven that he's ready to go onto the market, that he's ready to start cleaning up environmental hazards all over the world."

"And you're responsible for all of that," Dad said proudly.

I could only blink in amazement.

Suddenly, we were interrupted by another voice. "You'll get yours, McDoogle!"

I sat up on my elbows to see Mr. Snavely and his two buddies being hauled off toward a couple of police cars.

"You hear me, McDoogle?" he snarled. "You may have foiled our attempts this time, but you haven't heard the last of—"

That was as far as he got before one of the offi-
cers pushed his head down and helped him into
the car.

"Don't let him worry you," Dad grinned. "It'll be
a very long time before he gets out of prison."

"But why is he so mad at me?" I asked.

Doc laughed. "Because you're the hero. You're
the one who uncovered their plot. You're the one
who saved the city, saved my life, and proved Iatds
is ready for the real world. You did it all, Wally."

"But . . . But . . ."

"Just rest, Sweetheart," Mom said as she eased
me back down onto the gurney. "The next few days
are going to be pretty busy with the TV crews and
press conferences and everything."

"Press conferences?"

"That's right," Dad glowed. "Just like the doc
said, you're a hero."

"But . . . but all I did was . . . I mean, I just . . ."

"Bloomed where you were planted?" Mom asked
with a twinkle in her eye.

I looked at her more confused than ever. "Huh?"

"You just did what you could do where God
planted you."

I continued to stare.

"Think of it," she said. "If you had not gotten
the job working at the Water Management Facility,
none of this would have happened."

I closed my eyes trying to understand. She was right. None of this would have happened if I had been calling the shots my way, if things had gone how I wanted them to go. I couldn't believe it. True, it had gotten pretty dark there for a while, but in spite of that darkness, everything had turned out really, really bright.

"Okay folks," a young ambulance attendant said. "We need to take Wally here to the ER—the emergency room."

"The ER!" I choked. The truth is, going to hospitals makes me even more nervous than bad guys in bad suits, or crashing helicopters, or pollution-eating monsters."

"Don't worry," the attendant said. "We just need to run a few tests and make sure everything is okay."

"Absolutely," Dad agreed. "He's had a very traumatic time."

I turned to Dad. Was it my imagination or was there actually a catch in his voice? And then, the most amazing thing happened. He suddenly leaned forward, kissed me on the forehead, and said something I'd never heard before. At least not to me.

"Son," he tried to swallow back the emotion in his voice, "I'm proud of you. Real proud."

I had a lump in my throat the size of a basketball. All of my life Dad had wanted me to be "a real man," and all of my life I'd disappointed him. But now . . . well, I could only stare in amazement as the attendant unlocked the wheels to my gurney and started rolling me toward the ambulance.

"Oh, Wally." Dad hurried to catch up to us and brought ol' Betsy into view. "We found this at the Water Management Facility. I thought you might need it."

He set it beside me on the gurney. I gotta tell you. I thought my heart would nearly burst. Think of it, Dad was actually encouraging me to keep on writing. Would miracles never cease?

The attendant continued to roll me toward the ambulance as everyone promised to meet me at the hospital. But I barely heard their promises. Dad's words were still echoing in my head. And so were Mom's. "You just did the best you could where God planted you. If you hadn't got that job at the Water Management Facility none of this would have happened."

But she only knew a fraction of it. If I'd had my way, I wouldn't have taken the job in the first place, nor would I have ever met the "ghost," or got kidnapped by the suits, or crashed the helicopter, or nearly drowned, or been saved by Iatds. Amazing. It was like everything that I thought was so bad had actually worked out to be so good.

Incredible.

The attendant slid me into the ambulance. And, after joining me inside and shutting the doors, we were off. The ride would take about thirty minutes. And since I was feeling pretty good, and since I had to find some way to kill the time, I reached for ol' Betsy. After all, I wouldn't want to let Dad down.

I popped up the screen, snapped on ol' Betsy, and finished my superhero story.

When we last left Tidy Guy, his thoughts were messier than the cables in the back of a VCR. His thinking is so chaotic it doesn't even come out right on the page.

"Help

me!"

he cries,

"Help!"

me!"

The same goes for our baddest of
the bad guys:

YuG!

a!H

!oH   ydiT

!oH

Ha !   Up   iT,

gIve

And then, just when things couldn't
get any worse (or more confusing to
read), Chaos Kid reaches over to his
trusty chaos generator and begins dial-
ing dials, switching switches, and
flipping...er...flippers.

The generator roars louder and
louder and louder some more. Suddenly
the Chaos Beam explodes in a giant
flash of blinding light. Now everything is bathed in its mega messiness.
Everything loses order...planets,
people, even writers of superhero
stories.

"Hey, a minute wait!" I type. "That's
true not. Now out cut that! you hear
me, Do Kid Chaos? me Answer!"

A frightened Chaos Kid around looks and cries, "said that Who, who?"

"Me!" type I.

nervously, Fumbling for his generator, until down the power he turns the words I'm typing start to appear in the right order again. But Chaos Kid is still pretty frightened. Come to think of it, so is Tidy Guy.

"Who...who said that," Chaos Kid repeats as he searches the sky, obviously trying to figure out where my voice is coming from.

"Me," I type again.

He swallows hard. "Who's...who's 'me'?"

"Me. Your author."

"Our author?" Tidy Guy stammers.

"That's right."

Chaos Kid continues searching the heavens. "Listen," he shouts, "I don't care who you are. You can't just barge into our story like this."

"Says who?" I type.

"It's not fair. It doesn't make sense."

"That's right," I type. "If you want total chaos, then I can jump in and out of your story anytime I want."

"But it's not fair," Chaos Kid repeats. "I won't stand for it."

"You won't stand for it?" I type.

"That's right," he says, folding his arms and stomping his foot in defiance.

"Listen, Kid," I type. "If I wanted to, I could blow up the entire chaos generator by writing one sentence. Or for that matter, I could give you seventeen feet and three heads. Wanna see?"

"No, no!" he cries. "I believe you! I believe you!" He is definitely on the nervous side and takes a second to wipe his brow. He glances to Tidy Guy then looks back into the sky. "So what do we do now?" he shouts.

I type, "Now would be a good time for you to destroy your chaos generator and become Tidy Guy's friend."

"No way," Chaos Kid shouts.

He senses me reaching for the keyboard and, in a panic, shouts, "All right, all right. I'll do it! I'll do it!"

He turns to the generator and reluctantly starts to take it apart.

"Why did you build that thing in the first place?" Tidy Guy asks.

"Because the world doesn't make sense," Chaos Kid says. "It's nothing but chaos."

"That's not true," I type. "The world makes perfect sense."

"Not from here," he says. "From down here, a lot of stuff doesn't make sense."

"Maybe not to you," I type, "but from where I sit, everything does. Everything I type is for a reason. You may not understand it now, but believe me. When the story's over, it'll make perfect sense."

"That's pretty tough to believe."

I nod and type. "Guess you'll just have to trust me. Until then, I guess you'll have to bloom where I plant you."

"Yeah, but——"

"Listen," I interrupt, "we're getting close to the hospital so I better finish this. You guys go ahead, shake hands and make up."

Tidy Guy and Chaos Kid look at each other skeptically.

"Go on," I type. "Shake and make up."

Reluctantly, they reach out and shake
each other's hands.

"Good," I type.

I start to reach for the off switch
when Tidy Guy looks up and calls,
"Could you explain one thing?"

"What's that?"

"Why did I fly all the way over here
in my star cruiser, if you could have
stopped Chaos Kid on your own?"

I type, "Because I wanted you two
to meet and start working together."

"Really?" they both say in unison.

"Really," I type. "Tidy Guy, with
your sense of order, and Chaos Kid,
with your imagination, you two will be
able to do incredible things together."

"Hey," Chaos Kid beams, "I never
thought of that."

"Yeah," Tidy Guy grins, "that's
pretty cool."

"See," I type. "There are lots of
things you guys haven't thought of.
You'll just have to trust that I'm
doing stuff for good, even when it
doesn't look that way."

"Deal," Chaos Kid calls.

```
  "Deal," Tidy Guy agrees.
  "All right," I type, "I gotta go now.
We'll see you around."
  "Okay," they shout, "and good luck at
the hospital."
```

I reached over and shut ol' Betsy down just as the ambulance slowed to a stop in front of the ER entrance. Being at the hospital definitely made me nervous. But, just like Tidy Guy and Chaos Kid, I'd have to trust that God would work it out for my good. It's true, trusting isn't always easy, but I was making progress. Day by day, I was slowly making progress.

MY LiFe
as a
Bigfoot Breath Mint

Here's a little excerpt from my next book, My Life As a Bigfoot Breath Mint. *Lots of stuff happens, but at one point I get to drive one of those cool car rides at the famous movie theme park, Fantasmo World. Unfortunately, as you might guess, the park will never quite be the same again.*

The attendant gave us a running push and said, "Have a fan-fan-fantastic ride at Fantasmo World . . ."

And we were off.

What an experience. Feeling that powerful three-fourths horsepower engine throbbing under the hood. The wind flying through my hair. The blur of trees as we raced—

"C'mon, Wally," my little sister Carrie complained. "I can walk faster than this."

"All right, all right." I stomped on the accelerator. The raw power surged through the vehicle, the acceleration pushed us deep into our seats. Before I knew it, we were up to three and a half maybe even four miles an hour.

And then it happened. . . .

"Wally, what's wrong with that music?"

I gave a listen. It was the same neurotic theme song they'd been playing ever since we arrived:

> It's Fantasmo after all,
> It's Fantasmo after all,
> It's Fantasmo after all,
> It's a Fan-Fan-tasmo World.

But now it was going so fast it sounded like the Singing Chipmunks breathing helium. Faster and faster it played. Higher and higher the voices rose.

But it wasn't only the music that was going faster . . .

"Look at that!" I pointed.

Overhead, the sky ride was also picking up speed. Some of the people on board were starting to panic.

"And over there!" Carrie pointed to the nearby merry-go-round. It was spinning so fast that people were fighting to hang on. Everything was going faster. Everything including us.

"Slow down, Wally! Slow down!"

"I'm trying," I shouted as I hit the brakes for the hundredth time. But nothing happened.

Cars raced by. Some of the kids in them were screaming. Others crying.

"Slow down, Wally! You're scaring me!"

"I'm scaring *you*. What about *me!*"

The faster we went, the harder it was to steer. Now it's true, my eye-hand coordination isn't the best. In fact, I hold the world's record for the greatest number of quarters lost per video game. (Translation: I usually crash those jet fighter planes before they even get off the ground.) But this was ridiculous. If it weren't for that center bar running down the middle of the road, there was no way we could have stayed on the street.

And still we picked up speed.

Carrie began screaming. Non-stop. She didn't even take time out to breathe.

Faster and faster the road raced by.

Faster and faster my life flashed before my eyes.

And then I saw it. Actually, we both saw it.

"It's a hairpin corner!" Carrie screamed. "Turn, Wally, turn!"

"I'm turning. I'm turning."

I cranked that wheel as far to the left as possible. Unfortunately, the road turned to the right.

SCRAAAAAPE . . .
SCREEEEETCH . . .
K-BAM!

I'm not sure how it happened, but we were going so fast that our car jumped the metal bar in the center of the road and we flew off the track.

The good news was we were no longer on the highway ride that had gone berserk. The bad news was we were still in a car going berserk—going berserk and picking up speed.

First there were the usual bushes and shrubs:

K-THWACK, K-THWACK
"SCRRREEEEEEAAMMMMM!"

(Thank you, Carrie. I didn't need to use that ear again, anyway.) Now we were racing down the main thoroughfare. "Get out of the way!" I yelled. "Get out of the way! Get out of the—

K-SMACK, K-SMACK, K-SMACK!

Those, of course, were the slower moving pedestrians and—

"AUGGHHHH!"
RRIIIIIIIP . . .

the Galactic Space Queen dressed in long flowing robes. Well, she *had* been dressed in long flowing robes. Now they were trailing off our back bumper, and she was running for the nearest bushes.

But, the fun and games had barely begun.

"There's Daddy!" Carrie pointed. "And Burt and Brock!"

I spun around just in time to see them standing in a long line that we were zooming past.

And our brothers, being so kind and extremely intelligent, immediately began screaming, "Hey, no cuts! No cuts!"

I turned back to the front and saw why they were concerned. We were heading directly to the front of the most popular ride in the park . . . The Castle of Horrors.

You'll want to read them all.

THE INCREDIBLE WORLDS OF WALLY McDOOGLE

#1—My Life As a Smashed Burrito with Extra Hot Sauce

Twelve-year-old Wally—"The walking disaster area"—is forced to stand up to Camp Wahkah Wahkah's number one all-American bad guy. One hilarious mishap follows another until, fighting together for their very lives, Wally learns the need for even his worst enemy to receive Jesus Christ. (ISBN 0–8499–3402–8)

#2—My Life As Alien Monster Bait

"Hollyweird" comes to Middletown! Wally's a superstar! A movie company has chosen our hero to be eaten by their mechanical "Mutant from Mars!" It's a close race as to which will consume Wally first—the disaster-plagued special effects "monster" or his own out-of-control pride . . . until he learns the cost of true friendship and of God's command for humility. (ISBN 0–8499–3403–6)

#3—My Life As a Broken Bungee Cord

A hot-air balloon race! What could be more fun? Then again, we're talking about Wally McDoogle, the "Human Catastrophe." Calamity builds on calamity until, with his life on the line, Wally learns what it means to FULLY put his trust in God. (ISBN 0–8499–3404–4)

#4—My Life As Crocodile Junk Food

Wally visits missionary friends in the South American rain forest. Here he stumbles onto a whole new set of impossible predicaments . . . until he understands the need and joy of sharing Jesus Christ with others.
(ISBN 0–8499–3405–2)

#5—My Life As Dinosaur Dental Floss

It starts with a practical joke that snowballs into near disaster. Risking his life to protect his country, Wally is pursued by a SWAT team, bungling terrorists, photo-snapping tourists, Gary the Gorilla, and a TV news reporter. After prehistoric-size mishaps and a talk with the President, Wally learns that maybe honesty really is the best policy.
(ISBN 0–8499–3537–7)

#6—My Life As a Torpedo Test Target

Wally uncovers the mysterious secrets of a sunken submarine. As dreams of fame and glory increase, so do the famous McDoogle mishaps. Besides hostile sea creatures, hostile pirates, and hostile Wally McDoogle clumsiness, there is the war against his own greed and selfishness. It isn't until Wally finds himself on a wild ride atop a misguided torpedo that he realizes the source of true greatness. (ISBN 0–8499–3538–5)

#7—My Life As a Human Hockey Puck

Look out . . . Wally McDoogle turns athlete! Jealousy and envy drive Wally from one hilarious calamity to another until, as the team's mascot, he learns humility while suddenly being thrown in to play goalie for the Middletown Super Chickens! (ISBN 0–8499–3601–2)

#8—My Life As an Afterthought Astronaut

"Just 'cause I didn't follow the rules doesn't make it my fault that the Space Shuttle almost crashed. Well, okay, maybe it was sort of my fault. But not the part when Pilot O'Brien was spacewalking and I accidently knocked him halfway to Jupiter. . . ." So begins another hilarious Wally McDoogle MISadventure as our boy blunder stows aboard the Space Shuttle and learns the importance of: Obeying the Rules! (ISBN 0–8499–3602–0)

#9—My Life As Reindeer Road Kill

Santa on an out-of-control four wheeler? Electrical Rudolph on the rampage? Nothing unusual, just Wally McDoogle doing some last-minute Christmas shopping . . . FOR GOD! Our boy blunder dreams that an angel has invited him to a birthday party for Jesus. Chaos and comedy follow as he turns the town upside down looking for the perfect gift, until he finally bumbles his way into the real reason for the Season.
(ISBN 0–8499–3866–x)

#10—My Life As a Toasted Time Traveler

Wally travels back from the future to warn himself of an upcoming accident. But before he knows it, there are more Wallys running around than even Wally himself can handle. Catastrophes reach an all-time high as Wally tries to out-think God and re-write history. (ISBN 0–8499–3867–8)

Look for this humorous fiction series
at your local Christian bookstore.